If J.F.K. Had Lived: A Political Scenario

R. Reginald
and
Jeffrey M. Elliot

R. Reginald

the Borgo Press

San Bernardino, California
MCMLXXXII

Dedication of R. Reginald:
For my daughter, Lady Louise Rogers,
the lovely "Princess B," who will
always rule my political scenario.

Dedication of Jeffrey M. Elliot:
For Joseph R. Aicher, Jr.,
this small measure of my affection.

Library of Congress Cataloging in Publication Data:

Reginald, R.
   If J.F.K. had lived.

   Rev. ed. of: The attempted assassination of John F.
Kennedy. 1976.
   1. Kennedy, John F. (John Fitzgerald), 1917-1963—
Fiction. I. Elliot, Jeffrey M. II. Title.
PS3568.E4754A95 1982   813'.54   81-19516
ISBN 0-89370-155-6 (cloth)   AACR2
ISBN 0-89370-255-2 (paper)   OCLC #8032078

Produced, designed, and published by R. Reginald and
Mary A. Burgess, The Borgo Press, P.O. Box 2845, San
Bernardino, CA 92406, USA. Printed in the United States
of America by Victory Press, San Bernardino, CA. Binding
by California Zip Bindery, San Bernardino, CA. Cover
and title page design by Michael Pastucha.

First Edition———April, 1982

Introduction

"History is mostly guessing; the rest is prejudice."
—Will and Ariel Durant

* * *

What if? The perennial question. The unanswerable question. And yet, the question that remains. Why? Because each of us, regardless of position or circumstances, wishes, in some small or large way, that things might have worked out differently than they had. None of us is ever completely satisfied with the hand that history has dealt us. Likewise, it is this same question, "what if?," that motivates historians in their search for meaning and purpose in events past.

When asked with earnestness and dispassion, this is a valuable query, in that it often engenders increased understanding and awareness of historical processes. In answering it, we are forced to reexamine our values, attitudes, beliefs, assumptions, motivations, and actions, thereby broadening our perspective and expanding our worldview. We can never really be certain of what might have been, or what the consequences of any particular act might still be.

It is this question of alternatives which motivates the present work. In brief, it asks: What if John F. Kennedy had lived? What if he had survived his assassin's bullet? What if it was John Connally, and not he, who had been felled that tragic day? How would history have been different? Would our nation and the world be a changed place today? Would we be different as a people? Would we view ourselves and the world in new ways? Would our future today be filled with greater promise and opportunity? Would any of the problems that confront us, both at home and abroad, be alleviated? Would the world be filled with less ugliness, less hate, less violence? Would we as individuals feel better about ourselves, our nation, and the world?

This volume raises a number of other pertinent searching questions, among them: Was there something about John Kennedy that made him different from the presidents who preceded him and succeeded after him? Did he represent some special vision? Did he know something about us, as a people, that enabled him to marshal the best within us? Did he speak a universal language that transcended nations and ideologies? What was it about his death that made it so difficult to accept? Did a part of us die with him on that fateful day? Why is it so difficult, even today, to accept his death?

The present work does not pretend to answer all these questions. Indeed, it cannot. They defy easy or simple solutions. Instead, this volume approaches the subject from another perspective—namely, from the vantage point of historical fantasy. It asks the student to consider, if only for an hour or two, what might have happened had Kennedy lived to complete his term of office. It also explores deeper questions concerning forms of government, styles of rule, the wisdom of this nation's founders in establishing the government they did, and the cumulative effect that little actions might or might not have on the ensuing history of the world.

As you read this work, consider carefully the scenario presented. Draw upon your understanding of history. Make use of your knowledge of politics. Recall what you have read, heard, and witnessed. Turn back the pages of history. Examine the salient events that transpired. Listen to the words of those involved. Study the actions that were taken. And then ask yourself, "what if?" Does the scenario presented here make sense? Does it conform to known historical fact? Is it faithful to your reading of history? Suppose, just suppose, that the changes presented here had occurred. Would they have altered your life? The life of your country? The future of mankind? Would you prefer the seeming certainty of what took place to the uncertainty of what might have transpired? Finally, in the end, is history, as Napoleon Bonaparte has said, nothing more than "fable agreed upon?"

Jeffrey M. Elliot

If J.F.K. Had Lived:
A Political Scenario

MR. PETERSON: We want to thank you, Sir, for giving us this opportunity to interview you on the eve of your inauguration as James VII, Lord President of the United States of America. This is the Public Eye, a weekly television series spotlighting people in the news today. I'm your host, Myles Peterson, Washington correspondent for the Independent Broadcasting System; my colleagues for tonight's show are Dame Janet Harrington, columnist for the *Washington Digest*, and Hon. Steven Thomas, representing the Federal Cooperative Network. We will begin the questioning with the Hon. Mr. Thomas.

MR. THOMAS: Thank you, Myles. Lord President, you received an overwhelming popular mandate in the recent elections, some 74 percent of the votes cast, according to figures released by the independent National Polling Center. That's the highest percentage accorded a presidential candidate in the last hundred years. How do you think this unprecedented show of support will affect your proposed reorganization plans?

THE LORD PRESIDENT: Well, Steve, you and I both know that the public can change its mind almost as fast as a politician can. I appreciate very much the confidence shown me by the American people, and I'll do everything in my power to maintain it. That doesn't mean, however, that I'll shirk unpopular decisions when they have to be made, or avoid controversial issues just to keep those percentages up. I remember very well how Lord President John IV Kennedy started his administration with a high approval rating, and then watched it drop steadily as the Vietnam War dragged on. Presidents Richard I and Gerald I also suffered from "pollitis," Nixon because of Watergate and Freeman over the South African intervention. I think any Lord President has to expect that some of his decisions won't please all the people all of the time, and be willing to live with the consequences. I don't necessarily expect everyone to approve of everything I've done or will do; I do ask that they respect my good intentions and my integrity. I'll do the best I can for all Americans.

MR. THOMAS: To return to your proposals, sir; what do you think are your chances of getting them through Congress?

THE LORD PRESIDENT: (*pauses*)   Steve, these ideas of mine aren't particularly new or revolutionary, and I certainly haven't made any secret of them during my campaign. Presumably, those who voted for me were aware of my recommendations, and either approved of them, or at least didn't sufficiently disapprove to vote for my opponent. Now, I have to regard that kind of mandate as significant, and I think the House and Senate would be foolish to ignore the will of the people. We've just begun a new century, and we're long overdue for a few changes in the way we conduct our everyday business. The people have made it quite clear time and again during the last 26 years, ever since the Watergate Affair, that they want an honest, efficient government, and by God, I intend to make it so. Dame Harrington.

DAME HARRINGTON: Thank you, Lord President. All of Washington has been talking about the Under President-elect, the first black woman to be chosen for that office. How do you envision her role in the new government?

THE LORD PRESIDENT: Lady Jordan is amply qualified in every respect to assume the Lord Presidency, if that should be necessary, having had executive and legislative experience as a Congressperson, Senator, and Governor of the State of Texas. I wouldn't have chosen her if I'd felt otherwise. The problem I'm facing today is the problem faced by every Lord President of the last 50 years; now that I've got this multi-talented person on my staff, how do I best utilize her many skills? Part of this challenge is answered by my reorganization plan, which specifies in greater detail the role of the Under President, and expands his or her role to include additional duties in the legislative branch, or, at the option of the Lord President, appointment to a cabinet-level position, with actual administrative duties. This should help make her an integral part of my administration from the very beginning. Yes, Mr. Peterson.

MR. PETERSON: Sir, you'll be sworn in tomorrow as the 44th Lord President of the United States. What do you intend to tell the American people in your inaugural address?

THE LORD PRESIDENT: Well, Mr. Peterson, if I told you that, I wouldn't have much of anything to say tomorrow. And while that might make some of my opponents (and friends) happy, I'd prefer to wait until the occasion itself. I will say this, however: I think we need to restore America's faith in itself before we can restore its faith in government. My administration will be an honest one, and as efficient as we can make it.

MR. THOMAS: Lord President, we've talked in general terms about what you intend to do once you're sworn in; I wonder if we could begin discussing specifics.

THE LORD PRESIDENT: Please go ahead, Steve.

MR. THOMAS: Let's start first with foreign affairs. Relations with the United States of Europe have become strained in the last few years, beginning with the

Rouen incident.   How do you intend to improve our ties with the European nation?

THE LORD PRESIDENT: I have already made a tentative agreement to visit the U.S.E. in May of this year, beginning with a reception in Paris on the 16th.   King Henri VII of France will serve as host, and I understand the Lord Chancellor and Premier have expressed great interest in the prospect of meeting me the next day.   My itinerary also includes a stopover in London, on May 20th, which will commence with a visit to King Charles; I'll meet with Prime Minister Thorpe of England that evening, and with Prime Minister MacDonald of Scotland on the 21st.   During the next week, I'll be touring Belgium, The Netherlands, Denmark, and Norway.   The trip will end in West Germany, where I'm scheduled to confer with Kaiser Georg I and Baron Mueller on the 28th.   I'm hoping these personal contacts between governmental officials will lead to a new era of understanding between America and the U.S.E.   Incidentally, I've been invited to address the European Parliament in Brussels on May 30th.   Dame Harrington.

DAME HARRINGTON: Sir, as you see it, can anything be done about the present crisis in India?

THE LORD PRESIDENT: Well, Janet, I'm not really sure there's anything anyone can do at this point.   We have a situation here where the government has disintegrated into chaos, millions of people are starving, and China is threatening to move in.   The basic problem is one that the Government of India has overlooked all these years, and that's the population explosion.   India has steadfastly refused to accept reality, and to adopt measures to limit the size of its population.   The direct consequence of such irresponsibility is mass famine, and a gradual decline into barbarism.   I don't like to watch the news reports any more than you do, but I also don't like the idea of interfering in another country's internal affairs.   The United States no longer has the kinds of food surpluses it had back in the '60s and '70s, and I'm not willing to destroy what little reserves we have just to bolster the Indian government; and that's

8

all we'd be doing by sending them grain. As far as I can see, the situation is irretrievable: a great many people there are going to die, and there's absolutely nothing we can do about it at this point.

MR. PETERSON: Sir, we've heard a great deal about your career in the last few months, but none of the many reports on your life have really identified the beginnings of your interest in politics. Where did it start?

THE LORD PRESIDENT: You know, Myles, I'm not really too sure I can answer that one. When did you decide to become a reporter? These things are rarely clear cut, even in one's own mind. They tend to evolve over a period of years, as one gradually comes to the realization of what he or she wants to do. For me, I guess, my first moment of political awareness, if you want to call it that, was that dismal November afternoon 37 years ago when John Kennedy was shot in Dallas. I was just 16 at the time, attending high school in Spokane, Washington, and I remember very clearly the announcement coming over the loudspeaker. Shots had been fired at the Kennedy entourage, but nobody really knew what was going on. And then we heard that Kennedy himself had been wounded. It occurred to me suddenly how important one man could be, and how much difference it would make to the world if Kennedy died. There aren't very many men whose life or death could change history, but Kennedy was one of them, I was sure, and I was determined from that moment on to join that exclusive group if I could. The rest you know.

DAME HARRINGTON: Then your goal from the very outset of your career was the Lord Presidency?

THE LORD PRESIDENT: (laughs) I suppose that's the El Dorado of any politican. You start thinking of what you could do if you were sitting in that Oval Office, and you know you'll never be satisfied with anything less. Of course, you also realize that 99 percent of the population never get that far, that the odds are clearly stacked against you, and so you steel yourself against the ultimate disappointment. I find myself wondering sometimes how I ever managed to get here. It's like a dream to me—but a very pleasant one. Yes, Steve.

MR. THOMAS: During your campaign, you promised to pardon any draft evaders remaining at large from the South African intervention. Do you still intend to keep that pledge, after hearing the protests last week of the South African refugees in Arizona?

THE LORD PRESIDENT: It seems to me that the only way we can put the South African War behind us is by pardoning all the young men who fled the country or went underground to avoid doing what they felt was wrong. I don't deny that some of them were shirkers, and others may well have been cowards or mistaken in their judgments. I do say that it's time to lay such considerations aside, and forgive those who declined to participate in the most recent American intervention overseas. To that end, I will formally issue a presidential proclamation upon assuming office tomorrow, to insure that these young Americans are not branded as criminals by their country.

MR. PETERSON: Lord President, as part of my preparation for this interview, I've been reading all three of your published books relating to American politics, and I've been struck by your forceful analyses of recent history, and, in particular, your evident admiration of and sympathy for Lord President John IV Kennedy, a figure who has not been well-favored by most historians of modern times. What accounts for your high opinion of him?

THE LORD PRESIDENT: Well, Myles, I think he's been maligned, to be quite frank. Take the Cuban Missile incident, for example. Lord President Kennedy inherited a plan of action from his predecessor, Dwight I, that was based upon wrong information, and wrong suppositions, and was forced to act very quickly after assuming office, under great pressure from the military and the CIA. He made the wrong decision, obviously. We should not have attempted to invade Cuba, which had and has a right to choose its own government, whether or not we may approve of it. But Kennedy, unlike many leaders before and since, had the ability to admit his mistakes when he made them, and learn from his misjudgments, thereby growing in office. I like that kind of man.

MR. PETERSON: But surely, he made the same mistake again when he involved us in the Vietnam conflict. Or would you disagree?

THE LORD PRESIDENT: I would. Kennedy made the best decision he could with the information he had available. You must remember that even Lord Presidents aren't omniscient. They rely heavily upon their staffs, and the federal bureaucracy in general. In Kennedy's case, he derived his day-to-day information on the military situation in Southeast Asia from the Lord Field Marshall of the Armed Forces, his honorable cabinet officers, and his personal counselors, all of whom tended to view things in a particular way. And Kennedy himself was a man of action; he preferred to do something, and perhaps be forced to live with the consequences, than to do nothing. At the same time, he was an inexperienced administrator, having had few executive opportunities in the Senate, and was perhaps a bit naive. Everyone in government tends to regard his own position as important, usually more important than everyone else's, and everyone naturally tries to increase his or her importance in any way possible. The name of the game is power; the rules vary from person to person, but tend to be nonexistent near the top. Truth, what there is of it, is altered to suit the situation. Efficiency is less important than self-aggrandizement, job performance is judged primarily in terms of personal loyalty to one's superiors, and promotions nearly always result from expert boot-licking on the right occasions. No one sticks his neck out for any reason other than self-advancement. That's the way our government really operates, and it is, I admit, a somewhat cynical way of looking at things. Administrations may change, but the bureaucracy forever stays the same. It's very difficult to break through the circle of presidential advisers, even under the best of circumstances. Since they've all been appointed by the Lord President, they all tend to tell him or her exactly what he or she wants to hear. Simultaneously, they can easily become censors when the flow of information to the executive branch becomes so vast that it must necessarily be reduced to a manageable level; usually, that process is handled by the Lord President's staff; what he ultimately receives affects the way he thinks. I once read a story where a man set out to attain final power in his world. He progressively rose through the administrative ranks of his government, until he finally was elected to the Supreme Council, and was eventually chosen to be its leader. Then he discovered, much to his surprise, that the council based its decisions on information fed to it by a bank of computers, and only rarely deviated from the course indicated on the printouts. He traced the flow of information back down to a lowly clerical employee, who provided all the raw data from which the computer derived its formulations. The poor clerk was suddenly retired, and our hero was hired in his place, where he was finally in a position to affect the course of history. He lived happily ever after. There's a moral in that story for all of us. Kennedy escalated our involvement in Vietnam because he saw no other way out, based upon the data provided him. Once the U.S. was committed to a massive intrusion, a certain amount of self-justification set in at all levels of government, with a lot of wishful thinking. It's very easy to tell oneself, "just a little more, just a little longer, and we'll all be out of the woods." Unfortunately for everyone, it didn't happen that way. Eventually, one of the particpants had to bow out, and inevitably it had to be us, because the Vietnamese were not just fighting for political or philosophical ends, but for their homeland. As soon as you involve patriotism and nationalism in a war on one side, where the other side has nothing but political interests at stake, you immediately give the former an advantage, irrespective of war materiel. It took us many thousands of lives to realize that, and ultimately, it was the pragmatist, Lord President Richard I Nixon, who brought the troops home, not because he particularly wanted to, but because he had to if he ever wanted to get reelected. One somehow got the feeling that reelection was a large part of it. Mr. Thomas.

12

MR. THOMAS: You obviously have a mixed opinion of Lord President Richard I. Exactly how does he differ, in your estimation, from Kennedy, Carter, Reagan, or some of the more recent Lord Presidents, such as Sanders and Rogers?

THE LORD PRESIDENT: It seems to me, Steve, that a man is measured by the kinds of things he does in life. Everyone receives a certain share of opportunities, and luck, of course, plays its role in this; but luck has only a limited part in life, and a person has only himself to blame if he blows his chances. Nixon's a good example of how a person can go wrong in little ways. From the beginning of his term, he knew that he had the confidence of less than half the people, having been elected with just 43 percent of the vote. The Democrats controlled Congress, and although the Republicans made strenuous efforts throughout Nixon's term to gain a majority in the Senate, they didn't even come close. Combine these realities with the crises the U.S. was experiencing overseas, the riots and demonstrations at home, and we have a situation that was very difficult indeed. All of these danger signals should have been sufficient warning to keep a low profile and walk very softly and carefully around each problem. The country needed a soother, not a shouter, and Nixon failed to meet this challenge. By using a heavy hand wherever possible, he alienated millions of Americans. The way he employed Under President Agnew reflected credit on neither of them, and he surrounded himself with self-seeking advisers who virtually controlled the executive by restricting the flow of visitors and information. A crisis was inevitable.

MR. THOMAS: Of course, Lord President Nixon claimed to his dying day that he had no advance knowledge of the Watergate break-in, that he never condoned lawlessness among his staff, that the press manipulated the public into believing that he was guilty of crimes he never committed, or even knew about until after they were exposed.

THE LORD PRESIDENT: Still, he set the tone

13

for his administration. Look, Steve, if I hired you to guard my store—if I had a store—and if I came in one day to find that half the place was gone, I'd be justifiably angry, wouldn't I? Here I'd been paying you to watch over my goods, to protect my livelihood, and you had either been so lax that you failed to notice someone stealing them, or had fallen asleep on the job, or even worse, had been bribed to let someone take them. As a result, not only have I lost my investment, but also the money I'd been paying you. I'd have been better off if I'd simply bought myself a better lock. I feel the same way about Nixon. In the end, the worth of the man was revealed by the actions he took to ensure his reelection. Whether he knew the specific details really isn't as relevant as he seemed to think. I've never been particularly concerned about that part of it. What has always bothered me is the environment he created, in which semi-legal or even illegal acts were condoned or justified as part of the working atmosphere of his administration. His main rationale for all this seemed to be his own continuance in office, the kind of egoism that says a particular person is indispensable to the state. Towards the end of his term, everything else was subordinated to that one goal; increasingly, the many problems that required his attention were put aside, as he had to spend more and more of his valuable time fighting the slow, inexorable forces that were engulfing him. It was a sad case in every way. What made it even sadder was the man's obvious intelligence; Richard Nixon singlehandedly did more for American foreign policy than any Lord President in the preceding 20 years. Some of the impetus came from Baron Kissinger, of course, but he had to have the Lord President's backing and confidence to make even the slightest move towards the Chinese People's Empire, to cite just one example.

DAME HARRINGTON: I wonder if I could return to more immediate concerns, Sir.

THE LORD PRESIDENT: Yes, of course, Janet. Excuse me for rambling on; I enjoy talking, and it's very easy to get carried away.

14

DAME HARRINGTON: Sir, the right-to-life groups have been lobbying recently for a constitutional amendment to end voluntary euthanasia. Where do you stand on this issue?

THE LORD PRESIDENT: I'm against it, as I would be against any amendment that's legally unnecessary.

DAME HARRINGTON: But in this case, sir, the Lord Justices of the Supreme Court have struck down all laws restricting voluntary euthanasia. Wouldn't it take a constitutional amendment to restore the ban?

THE LORD PRESIDENT: That's true, Janet, but I am unalterably opposed to amendments that restrict the individual's right to do what he or she pleases with his or her own body. We had a similar situation 20 or 30 years ago, when another group of misguided individuals attempted to amend the Constitution to prohibit abortions. Personally, I find abortions repugnant, from nearly every possible perspective; if you're going to practice birth control, the time to do it is beforehand, not afterwards. But if someone wants to have an abortion, I don't think the government ought to interfere. I'm not saying, mind, that everyone *must* have an abortion, and I'm not even saying that every doctor must participate; what I am saying is that it should be a matter of personal choice. Those who find it morally reprehensible need not participate, and if they can convince the rest of society that their views are right and just, so be it. But let's not write such convictions into the Constitution, which was never designed as a moral arbiter. As it happened, the abortion groups were never able to convince a majority of the American people that their position was right, and the proposed amendments failed. I hope and trust the same thing will happen today.

DAME HARRINGTON: The euthanasia groups say they're only attempting to outlaw legal murder.

THE LORD PRESIDENT: Is it moral, then, to make unreasonable efforts to sustain life even when there's no possibility that the person involved will ever be able to function as a human being again? That kind of argument angers me. We now have machines that will continue bodily functions indefinitely; scientists have told me that theoretically they can keep us going for 50 to 100 years beyond the normal life span of Homo sapiens. But is it right to do so? You see, the one problem with this entire business is that we haven't yet found any way of slowing down or arresting the decay of the mind, the one thing that distinguishes men from brute animals. They can replace all the parts except that one, and that's the only one that really matters. I'd rather not live than live to be a 150-year-old vegetable. If I can't enjoy life, why bother? Mr. Peterson, you've been rather quiet for the past few moments.

MR. PETERSON: Not intentionally, sir, let me assure you. An item on the service wires last week indicated that Nigeria had become the 45th nation to explode an atom bomb. What do you think can be done to halt the proliferation of nuclear weapons?

THE LORD PRESIDENT: At this point, nothing. Too many countries have them, and too many others could have them if they wanted them. A college student could make one, if he had the raw materials. The time for reasonable efforts at control has long since passed. I would welcome more signatures on the various test ban treaties that have been put forward in the last 30 years, but practically, I see no way of enforcing them short of war, and that's precisely what these treaties are supposed to prevent.

MR. THOMAS: People's Tsar Sergei I Tigranovich said in a speech New Year's Day that he would welcome better Soviet-American relations. What are your feelings on this subject?

THE LORD PRESIDENT: Pretty much the feelings of all Americans, I think: we would all welcome better relations with all our earthly neighbors. The question is, does the government of the United Soviet Socialist Empire really want better relations, or are they just saying

16

so to gain a short term advantage in a long term struggle? Judging from past experiences, I'd be very hesitant to accept too much of what the Soviets say on face value, although I welcome the People's Tsar's speech, and I hope that we can meet personally after I take office.   Dame Harrington.

DAME HARRINGTON: Sir, I've read all of your books.   Have you written anything beside political studies?

THE LORD PRESIDENT: In my younger days, I wrote some fiction and verse. But I don't do much any-more; it requires more time and concentration than I can afford to give it, and I'd rather not do anything unless I can do it right.

DAME HARRINGTON: You   wrote   poetry? Could you give us an example of your work?

THE LORD PRESIDENT: Well, I could try, if you really want to hear something. (*murmers of approval*) Very well, then; this is one of my favorites. It has no title:

> *Your heart is open to mine eyes, as clear*
> *Before me as your face recumbent on*
> *My shoulder. I can feel your warmth, and hear*
> *The sigh of your breath.   There's a smile upon*
> *Your lips. But still the demons trouble me,*
> *And bid me look again. "Those lines," they say,*
> *"Those crooked scars of time; when will they flee*
> *Away?" And yet I love you. When I weigh*
> *The cumbrances of age against the love*
> *You give so freely, how can I resist?*
> *You've renewed my spirit, partaken of*
> *My life, and made of me your loyalist.*
> > *Then why these doubts that nothing can dispel?*
> > *I know your heart too little—or too well!*

ALL: Thank you, Lord President.

MR. THOMAS: Sir, if we could get back to business . . .

THE LORD PRESIDENT: Of course, Mr. Thomas.

MR. THOMAS: Well, sir, the United Party still controls the House of Representatives, and I was wondering if you anticipate any difficulties working with the leadership there.

THE LORD PRESIDENT: Steve, I'm always willing to meet with the leaders of the House, on any occasion where it might be of use. And I don't think I'll prove inflexible, either on legislative matters, or anything else. On the other hand, I am making some serious and well-considered proposals for governmental reorganization, and I expect them to receive the attention they deserve. I will be most happy to work with any member of either party in the House or Senate to get these proposals passed intact.

MR. PETERSON: Different Lord Presidents have handled their relationships with the press in different ways. What will Lord President James VII do?

THE LORD PRESIDENT: Well, I hope he'll do a little better job than some of his predecessors (*laughter*) Seriously, Myles, I think that good relations with the press are extremely important to any public figure—that's why I'm meeting with you here tonight—and I intend to do the best I can to make them cordial and easy-going at all times. I hope to hold regular press conferences every other Monday morning at ten o'clock, except when I'm out of town on business or vacation. One reporter from every major news agency will be given permanent status, and the rest will be rotated by lot. Questions will be allowed on all subjects, although I don't necessarily guarantee an answer to every one of them. If I don't like the questions, believe me, I'll tell you so.

MR. THOMAS: I'm sure you will, sir. Imperial Leader Wang Min-t'ang of the Chinese People's Empire is visiting the Kingdom of Hawaii this week, seeking to renew the ties established five years ago between Honolulu and Peking. King Kalakaua III has reassured the Chinese leader of the eternal friendship between Hawaii and Peking, and has pledged his assistance in overthrowing the government of the Kingdom of Taiwan. What's your reaction to his statement?

THE LORD PRESIDENT: China and Hawaii are perfectly free, in my opinion, to do as they please, so long as they don't immediately threaten the security of the United States. Talk is just that, and as long as it remains talk, I foresee no difficulties in relations with either country. Certainly, Hawaii has had reason to be wary of American policy since a group of American merchants tried to overthrow the monarchy there in 1893. Fortunately, Lord President Stephen I Cleveland intervened, and restored Queen Liliuokalani to her throne later that same year. Every other attempt to annex the islands to this country has been defeated, and rightfully so. The United States has no claims or designs upon the Kingdom of Hawaii, and hopes to continue its cordial relations with that country indefinitely, as reaffirmed by the Treaty of Hilo, signed by Lord President Thomas II Wilson and Queen Kaiulani in 1918.

DAME HARRINGTON: Do you have any comments to make concerning the outgoing administration of Lord President Richard II Rogers?

THE LORD PRESIDENT: Not really, Janet; I think it would be inappropriate for me to comment upon the man I'm replacing. History will render its judgment in due course, but it would be somewhat precipitous on my part to begin compiling that record now. I will say that I've had very good relations with the Lord President since being elected, and I respect his opinions very highly. They've been based, after all, on a great deal of practical experience, the kind only eight years in office can bring.

MR. THOMAS: Do you intend to run for reelection four years hence?

THE LORD PRESIDENT: Provided that my health remains good, and I haven't fallen flat on my face in the interim, you can count on it.

DAME HARRINGTON: The price of gas this morning at my local service station was $15.61 per liter. What hope can you offer the American people for an end to the energy crunch?

THE LORD PRESIDENT: Immediately, not much, I'm afraid. This is a longstanding problem that was ignored for several decades, years when we should have been looking for solutions. There are no panaceas. The fact of the matter is that we're running out of oil, that it's getting more and more difficult to find and process; the price will continue to rise as oil gets scarcer. Almost every well in the western world is dry; we still have some reserves of oil shale, but even that will be exhausted within another ten or fifteen years. The Arabs are pumping reserves, not new finds. The program instituted by Lord President Richard II to convert garbage, weeds, and crop scraps into natural gas *has* kept us from having aother disastrous winter like the one of '92, when over a thousand people froze to death in the northern part of this country; that together with our coal reserves and the conscientious reforesting of various park areas, should keep Jack Frost from our door for the foreseeable future. I'll not have our citizens go cold. The continued migration of our people from north to south has helped also. The conversion of locomotives from diesel to coal-generated steam power will proceed apace under my administration; I expect all of them to be converted or re-placed within two years. I will ask for legislation banning the few remaining internal combustion engine cars from the road; only electric vehicles will be allowed in the future. Bicycling will be encouraged. The solar cell stations in the southwestern deserts will be expanded, as will wind mach-ines where appropriate, tidal generators, steam taps through the Earth's crust, and general conservation measures. However, scientific experts assure me that the only longterm solution to this problem lies in one of two directions: nuclear fusion or solar energy beamed directly from stationary satellites parked in Earth orbit. Both of these will require much more research to implement, and both have enormous ecological and other problems associated with them. Nonetheless, I shall propose to Congress in my first legislative package that we fund investigations into both areas. Since we already have several space stations permanently on duty, the beamed energy concept seems to me more feasible; I will urge N.A.S.A. to develop detailed plans for implementation at the earliest possible date.

You know, Lord President James VI has been castigated for being a weak, vacillating executive who accomplished nothing during his four years in office except getting thirty Americans trapped in Iran. This picture does him a considerable wrong, in my estimation, because he was the only Lord President during a twenty-year period who publicly recognized that there was an energy problem, that we would all pay the price someday soon, and that we had better start thinking about the alternatives, alternatives the American public did not want to face. So, like Cassandra, he was ignored, given an early retirement, and shuffled off to Georgia. Then in the late '80s we suddenly realized that the oil glut was over, this time for good, and that there were no alternatives except severe dislocations, privation, discomfort (sometimes to the point of death), and starvation in the less fortunate countries of the world. We have no one to blame but ourselves. I will repeat again: there are no easy answers, no easy ways out. There are solutions to these problems, but they will be expensive, difficult to achieve, and disruptive. We will continue to change our patterns and styles of living; some of these changes will not be very palatable. Even now, most households can no longer afford plastic goods. We must adopt a permanent philosophy of conservation, recycling as much as possible, keeping wasteful consumption to a minimum. I will institute such measures where I can in government, and where I can in my own household. Mr. Peterson.

MR. PETERSON: Do you have any comments on the recent military coup in Bulgaria?

THE LORD PRESIDENT: The United States will not interfere with internal matters in the Kingdom of Bulgaria. The transference of rule from the communist governments of eastern Europe to military dictatorships has been a long-standing trend there, ever since the Polish crisis of the early 1980s. The communist system has been breaking down for some time, and seems at this point to be in far worse shape, both economically and politically, than the western states. I regret this, since it means great suffering for the peoples of eastern Europe, but I do not see that we can do much about it. Russia has been predicting for many decades the imminent collapse of capitalism; perhaps it should be more concerned with keeping its own house in order. Incidentally, the government of King Simeon II has not asked for our help in restoring order.

DAME HARRINGTON: Sir, the minimum retirement age was once again boosted by Congress last year to 80, and social security benefits adjusted accordingly. Do you think this is fair to those who have paid into the system all their lives?

THE LORD PRESIDENT: No. But I don't know either where we are going to find the money to pay for a reduced age limit. Unfortunately, with the birth rate continuing to decline, and the average age of the population continuing to increase, we don't really have much choice in the matter—we either increase the retirement age or reduce benefits. The private systems are experiencing similar problems. All of this is not new, of course; the retirement "problem" has been with us for the last two decades. The structure of the social security system demands increasing numbers of young people to finance the system on an ongoing basis for the elderly recipients; we haven't had such numbers for many years, and changes will continue to be made as needed.

DAME HARRINGTON: But Sir, don't you run the risk of alienating the Gray Lobby?

THE LORD PRESIDENT: If any of them have a

22

better solution, I'd be happy to hear it. Somebody has still got to pay the bills, and I'm ultimately responsible for seeing that everything works.

MR. THOMAS: Unemployment now stands at 17 percent of the national workforce, interest rates have been running at about 25 percent, and the gross national product has declined for ten quarters in a row. Would you not regard these as depression-level statistics, and what do you intend to do about them?

THE LORD PRESIDENT: These are the statistics, obviously, which got me elected, despite the fact that I have again promised no easy solutions. The economy has not been "well" by normal indicators since the first oil crisis in 1973, although various graphs have fluctuated wildly up and down as we have gone through minibooms and minibusts, with the busts predominating. Interest rates have not sunk below 10 percent since 1980. The national debt now stands at ten trillion dollars. All of these problems build on one another, none are easy to solve, and many now seem insoluble, given the present world circumstances. The heart of the matter is, of course, the high cost of energy; another difficulty is the reluctance of government and the citizenry to accept inevitable reductions in their standards of living. We have all been living beyond our means for a great many years. We're spoiled, to put it bluntly. We must collectively rid ourselves of many bad habits, or face some catastrophic collapse not too many years hence. I intend to appoint a broadly-based commission to examine this problem, with a reporting date three months hence, and ask these economic, social, and political experts to come up with some solutions that they can agree upon; whether we, both government and people, can accept what I expect to be hard tidings remains to be seen. The economy has been the downfall of every Lord President since Nixon; having seen all those men fail, more or less, at solving some very basic problems, makes me pessimistic that they will be rectified overnight. We must somehow try to restore the confidence of the people in both the government and the economy.

MR. PETERSON: To return to the energy situation for a moment, sir, I wonder if you could comment on the increasing levels of air pollution and acid rain generated by the nationwide conversion to coal-burning power plants and industrial facilities, and coal-powered steam engines.

THE LORD PRESIDENT: By 1990, every lake in the northeastern part of this country and the eastern part of Canada was ecologically dead due to acid rain; this abated somewhat in the early 1990s, as industrial facilities were shut down by the sudden scarcity of oil, and a few of these bodies of water began showing signs of life again. Unfortunately, the conversion to coal as our major source of energy has sparked an increase in the acid levels of rain over the last few years. Air pollution, which had abated considerably by 1995, is rising again, particularly in the East. Ironically, California now has some of the best air quality levels in the country, but California also has perhaps a third of the solar energy stations. I will make an effort to provide governmental assistance to power plants and general industry to reduce pollution to a livable level, if Congress will provide the funds. Air pollution throughout the world has been increasing steadily over the past decade, as third world countries have turned heavily towards wood, charcoal, peat, and dung as their major sources of available energy.

MR. PETERSON: If I may ask a follow-up question relating to this topic, the recently-released census figures show another large population shift to the sun belt, with population in the northern states actually decreasing by 10 percent over a ten-year period. Do you see this trend continuing, and what does it mean to the country as a whole?

THE LORD PRESIDENT: Well, it means that people are voting with their feet, showing that they don't have much confidence in the ability of government to keep them warm at prices the ordinary citizen can afford. I can't say that I blame them. For the national government, and for the local and state governments in both areas, it means horrendous problems—the northern states and big cities are continuing to lose their tax bases, just at a time when they

24

need every penny they can find; the southern states and their cities are unable to provide services for the new arrivals. These internal immigrants often can't find jobs or housing in the overcrowded sun belt, so they wind up in tent cities and makeshift trailer parks on the outskirts of the large metropolitan suburbs, loading the welfare rolls beyond all capacity, increasing crime statistics, overloading school systems at a time when all governmental budgets are declining. Yet there's very little we can do about it without becoming tyrants, and shipping them off to camps, or sending them back north against their wills. There's no money to build government-subsidized housing, like they did back in the '70s; there's no money for jobs programs. The economy of Southern California can't handle two million plus new immigrants a year, which is what they're getting. The population of Los Angeles and its suburbs now approaches forty to fifty million citizens; the San Diego area stands at twenty million. Miami, Florida, even taking into account the disastrous hurricane of ten years ago, now has twenty-five million men, women, and children. Dallas Worth, Texas, stands at thirty million. Even Albuquerque now has a population exceeding ten million. These figures, when actually translated into living human beings, provide problems of control that are almost insurmountable. We'll do the best we can under the circumstances, but don't expect miracles.

DAME HARRINGTON: Sir, what about illegal immigrants?

THE LORD PRESIDENT: Since the U.S. southern borders were closed in 1989, we've had very little problem with illegal immigrants from the Empire of Mexico; the bilateral treaty signed between Emperor Maximiliano II and Lord President Albert I in that year provided for a permanent, formidable border barrier patrolled on both sides, in return for American legalization of marijuana, with Mexico designated as the exclusive supplier. In recent years, however, we've had considerable problems with illegal immigration from the Kingdom of Canada, primarily due to the scarcity and high price of fuel when matched with Canada's unusually cold climate. I intend to hold talks with King Richard and Prime Minister Wickheizer at the earliest possible moment to discuss the situation, and see if we can come to an agreement; I will also meet with Queen Marie of Quebec and Premier Mauzee whenever and wherever they are willing.

MR. THOMAS: Lord President, it has been suggested by certain members of the opposition party that now is the time to reduce expenditures on the military; what is your reaction to this statement?

THE LORD PRESIDENT: I'd be glad to, if it were possible. Unfortunately, with both the Russians and Chinese now building permanent space bases on the Moon and in Earth orbit, I don't see that we have much choice but to meet them man for man, weapon for weapon. Any other course means the effective abdication of our role as a major power, as well as long-term economic disaster if we are frozen out of the search for raw materials in the solar system. Whoever controls space also controls the Earth below it; if no one controls space, we all do, in effect. I intend to see that we maintain our presence there permanently, at whatever cost. The U.S. Space Force is still small, but highly trained and motivated. Yes, Dame Harrington.

DAME HARRINGTON: Every Lord President of recent memory has had problems with certain members of his administration becoming involved in somewhat scandalous activities of one sort or another; if this happens to you, how will you deal with this problem?

THE LORD PRESIDENT: I'll pray a lot. (*everyone laughs*) Seriously, I don't want to buy trouble by anticipating things that probably won't come about. If one of my staff or administration does misbehave, I hope I'll have the courage to face it directly. I won't hesitate to dismiss someone who's out of line, or order the prosecution of any staff member who has done something illegal. At the same time, I hope I'll give anyone accused of wrongdoing a chance to prove him- or herself innocent. There's a fine line here that a few (nameless) Lord Presidents have crossed,

26

and others have recognized; let's hope we all have the wisdom to act as if we had hindsight. Being human, I don't guarantee that, of course.

MR. THOMAS: Do you support public transportation?

THE LORD PRESIDENT: I have already instructed my cabinet to prepare a plan for the reelectrification of urban railway systems in the large metropolitan areas. With the vast reduction in the numbers of automobiles on the highways, now confined primarily (and soon exclusively) to electric-powered cars, we now have a large number of almost-deserted roadways that can be converted to trolleys and electric-powered buses. These would be much less expensive than subway systems. There are some existing railroad tracks in urban areas that could also be converted into throughways for passenger vehicles.

MR. PETERSON: Sir, your nomination of Dr. Eliot Goldberg for the State Department has created a certain amount of controversy, since he has no previous diplomatic experience; could you comment on this?

THE LORD PRESIDENT: I have every confidence in Dr. Goldberg's abilities, both as a diplomat and as a man; I expect to leave him an exhausted man eight years from now.

MR. PETERSON: I'd like to return for a moment to Lord President Kennedy, if I might.

THE LORD PRESIDENT: Certainly, Myles.

MR. PETERSON: There are some who say the CIA was involved in the shooting at Dallas in 1963, that a massive conspiracy was responsible for planning the entire incident. Certainly, the killing of Lee Harvey Oswald so soon after he was arrested seems suspicious. Do you have any comments to make about the Kennedy shooting?

THE LORD PRESIDENT: This is ancient history, of course. This particular theory has never been proved or disproved, and quite frankly, I doubt that it will ever be. If indeed there was a conspiracy, those involved in its workings were certainly clever enough to dispose of the evidence a long time ago, and probably are dead; it's extremely unlikely that anything further will surface now. The fact that proponents of the theory have failed to corroborate any of their central conclusions seems, in my mind, to lessen its validity. Public figures are really very easy types to kill, because they all follow regular schedules, with lots of publicity; and by killing one of them, a person immediately gains a certain notoriety. Just as the Lord Presidency itself is the most sought-after position in the country, so too is the killing of a Lord President the height of infamy. There's a certain warped logic that says, if you're going to do it, you might as well start at the top. For certain types of people, those misfits who've never been able to find their niche in life, such notoriety is the most they can ever hope for. What I'm saying is that it's quite conceivable that one man could have shot Kennedy; it's much less likely that more than one did, since every additional person involved in a plot is one more who could spill the beans. As far as the CIA is concerned, or any other governmental agency, there's never been any evidence to suggest that they plotted the death of their Commander-in-Chief. Yes, Steve.

MR. THOMAS: Isn't it true, though, that many of the persons who witnessed the shooting died shortly thereafter?

THE LORD PRESIDENT: Some did, some didn't; some are even alive today. It's like the curse of Tutankhamen's tomb, back in the 1920s: a pharaoh's final resting place is uncovered and immediately a number of persons involved in the discovery start falling over. Was there a curse? Or was it just the fancies of idle minds trying to find logical explanations for things which require none? You tell me. A large number of conspirators would have made some mistakes; if there had been a plot behind Ken-

28

nedy's shooting, certainly it would have come out over the years. Yet, it never has.

DAME HARRINGTON: Lord President, to change the subject once again, your daughter has been reported living unmarried with a man in Seattle. How do you feel about such relationships?

THE LORD PRESIDENT: When I was growing up, I had a number of friends who shacked up with their girlfriends, so it doesn't really shock me in the least, if that's what you're asking. My daughter's a grown woman, and she's free to do what she likes with her life. I'd be the last person in the world to try and tell her what to do—and she'd be the last to listen, I think. I neither approve nor disapprove. If she loves the young man, that's good enough for me, and I'll respect her choice. Whether or not she goes through the marriage ceremony is something she must decide; certainly the measure of one's affection for another person lies not in such mundane things as rings, flowers, or vows, but inside the heart: all the weddings in the world won't increase one's feelings one iota unless that person already cares. I've known many married couples whose lives were one long hell; conversely, I've known unmarried pairs who were radiantly happy. I think you ought to leave people alone to live their lives as they see fit, and interfere with them as little as humanly possible.

MR. PETERSON: You've said on many occasions that one of your first acts in office will be tax reform. What do you think is wrong with the present system?

THE LORD PRESIDENT: Just about everything, Myles. The whole tax structure is basically unfair, because it places a greater burden on those least able to pay. In theory, it's supposed to work the other way around, but over the years so many loopholes have been added by special interest groups and rich lawyers that the result is so much Swiss cheese: it's full of holes. I want a reasonable tax structure, with no exceptions, no outs for anyone, no misunderstandings of what anyone owes. I don't even particularly care precisely how it's set up, or what the rates are, so long as they're uniformly and fairly applied. Just because Jack Smith's a dogcatcher doesn't mean that he should receive a special exemption for flea powder, even if it's necessary to his job. That's a ridiculous example, of course, but there are just as many ridiculous examples that have actually been put into law.

MR. THOMAS: Although the facts have been published many times, I wonder if you could tell us in your own words something about your career in public office.

THE LORD PRESIDENT: Well, Steve, I graduated from Gonzaga University in 1969, was drafted by the Army, and served two years, one in Vietnam. That was 1970, as I recall. Fortunately, I came through without much damage to limb or mind, although I saw some pretty gruesome things over there. War is not a gentle business, and both sides had flashes of excessive brutality.

MR. THOMAS: Did you actually participate in any of the fighting?

THE LORD PRESIDENT: Yes and no. I was trained as a medic, and was stationed for the most part in base areas. There were several occasions, however, when I was involved in skirmishes, and at least one time, I remember picking up a gun to defend myself. But everything happens so fast in battle that it's difficult afterwards to remember the exact sequence of events. I was lucky; some of my friends weren't so lucky.

MR. THOMAS: When did you first become involved in politics?

THE LORD PRESIDENT: Actually, I first became involved while still attending school. Neither Gonzaga nor Spokane, Washington, could have been regarded as hotbeds of political fervor, at least not when compared to the rest of the nation at that time; the "Jebbies," as we called the Jesuit fathers, tended to keep things pretty well

30

under control. I ran for school office several times, even got elected as Under President of the Senior Class, and then became involved with Robert Kennedy's bid for the Democratic nomination.

MR. THOMAS: What exactly did you do?

THE LORD PRESIDENT: Very little, when I think of it. (*laughter*) We did all the usual things you do in a campaign that both annoy and interest people; we made the rounds of neighborhoods, passed out our literature, phoned endless numbers of registered Democrats, and generally made nuisances of ourselves. I still wonder to this day if Kennedy would have gotten the nomination had he lived. But, of course, he was shot in Los Angeles early in June, about the same time I graduated, and the shock of his death, combined with my induction notice a year later, effectively removed me from the scene.

MR. THOMAS: Then you went off to war. When did you return to politics?

THE LORD PRESIDENT: In a way, I don't suppose I ever left it. Even though I was out of the country for two years, first in West Germany and then in Vietnam, I was well aware of what was happening here. I heard how former Under President Lyndon Johnson, for example, managed to secure the nomination after Robert Kennedy's death, and the close election results in the fall, when Richard Nixon just beat him out by a hair. The difference, I suppose, was that I heard it all at a distance, once-removed, rather than close at hand, as a participant. But I tried to keep informed. And my political education proceeded dramatically on another front, one that I'd never really experienced before, with my introduction into Army politics. You have to realize, Steve, that the Army is just another bureaucracy, in its own way, and that the oil of all bureaucracies is political favors; it's a lesser form of the pay-off systems you see so rampant in the Middle East, and in socialized bureaucracies, like the Soviet Union. Instead of cash changing hands, an intricate system of political I.O.U.'s and debits is used to buy services one might normally expect to receive. In that sense, I suppose, we're somewhat more sophisticated than the Arabs; we use checks instead of money rolls. Well, I can recall being stationed at a base in West Germany, where a hard-bitten old sergeant had somehow managed to get control of base leaves, and doled them out one by one to anyone who could pay the price. That price varied from man to man, depending on the person's position, rank, and influence. This sergeant had the best-stocked larder in town, because every time one of the cooks wanted to go off base, cakes, meats, and other special treats would somehow find their way into this guy's hoard. And he was completely amoral about the whole thing; you either paid whatever price he wanted, or you just didn't go anywhere. He could care less whether or not you had a legitimate reason for taking off, or whether you actually had earned your leave. No tickee, no washee. He was probably the most hated man on base, the C.O. included, but no one was ever able to break the stranglehold he held in that one key position. In the end, he was transferred out, but before leaving, he actually sold off his office to the highest bidder, and then made sure that his designated heir really succeeded him. This experience taught me two things: evil people do exist; an honest politician accepts no gifts. It occurred to me at the time that this mercenary sergeant, although immensely powerful, hadn't the faintest idea of what to do with his power except feather his own nest. What a waste of talent! Here was a man who could have added a great deal to the Army, and instead he used his abilities to prey on a bunch of poor bastards who had almost nothing to begin with. He was a parasite in uniform. You may well wonder why the C.O. didn't clamp down on this guy, and toss him out. Well, I found out afterwards from a friend who stayed in the service that the general in charge of the base used this sergeant to help keep in line a few men who didn't like to play the game the way the general wanted it played. Anyone who didn't applaud loudly enough when the general stepped out of the shower found himself given the runaround any time he wanted to do something that required formal permission from higher authority.

MR. THOMAS: But surely, Lord President, yours was a unique experience.

THE LORD PRESIDENT: I wish I could say so, Steve, but this kind of creeping corruption seems to permeate every bureaucracy, governmental or otherwise, that I've ever been associated with. It's a moral disease, utterly insidious in its effects, spreading slowly but inexorably from person to person in the hierarchical structures of bureaucratic systems. Those who manage to throw off the infection are inevitably scarred by it, and just enough succomb to keep it going. Let's consider, for a moment, a hypothetical situation. A certain Mr. Thomas is hired into a low-level administrative job by a public agency. This Mr. Thomas happens to be rather more astute than the average Joe, and within a few months he figures out how the game is played. He is immediately faced with a dilemma: does he go along with it, or does he refuse? Because, you see, he discovers that his boss is the kind of guy who doesn't particularly bother with such things as ethics, morals, or doing a good job; those kinds of concerns aren't related to political survival, at least in the eyes of his boss, and so they don't matter very much when matched against such "virtues" as personal loyalty, kowtowing, and bootlicking. There are a number of senior executives in this agency who have rather obviously sold out, since they wouldn't have gotten where they are otherwise; they're mediocre workers, and seem to know relatively little about the jobs they're supposed to be supervising, but they all have one outstanding quality in common: they're intensely loyal to the man who put them there, and they'll do anything that's asked of them. Now, as I said, our Mr. Thomas is somewhat more discerning than most, and he notices a curious thing, what I'll call the "King Henry effect." King Henry VIII, you will recall, ruled England in the 16th century—he was the one with six wives. In those days, monarchs were absolute rulers of their states; they could do just about anything they pleased, and there was no one to say nay. This wasn't enough for Henry; he also wanted his subjects' willing and wholehearted approval, and not giving one's approval was in itself grounds for treason. Sir Thomas More kept silent about the King's marriage; Henry wanted his acquiescence, as signified by the loyalty oath imposed upon all state officials; when More declined to swear, he was brought to trial on drummed-

33

up charges supported with false evidence, and promptly executed. Mr. Thomas's administrator is this kind of man, who not only wants to have his way, but also demands the applause of his employees. And Mr. Thomas refuses to applaud, although he does his job in every detail to the best of his ability, performs any tasks directly assigned to him, and is, in every other respect, a model employee. The result: Mr. Thomas, although he's retained in his position, will never advance beyond a relatively low level, despite good and loyal service to the state. He chooses to do that rather than compromise his principles. And yet he is injured to some degree, because all persons want the approval of their fellow beings; and he feels, with some justification, that his talents have been ignored, his good service denigrated, his abilities slighted. His morale declines, his performance levels drop, and he starts looking for a way out, either another job, or a transfer to an equivalent position else-where in the system. Thus, the good employee is penalized for his good qualities, and the political hack tends to advance to the top; there seems to be no easy way to change the situation without somehow dismantling the bureaucratic structure that furthers the system. I seem to have gotten a little off the subject, Steve; perhaps you can direct me back to my topic.

MR. THOMAS: We were talking about your career, sir. What did you do after the war?

THE LORD PRESIDENT: I was sent to Viet-nam about the time that Nixon was sworn in as Lord President, and spent almost a year there, being released just prior to Christmas of 1971. When I returned, I enrolled in law school at the University of Southern California, and three years later passed the bar exam. At about this time, the Watergate mess was coming out, and once more I found myself absorbed in current history.

MR. THOMAS: You've already indicated your mixed feelings regarding Lord President Richard I; where do you think he went wrong?

THE LORD PRESIDENT: Perhaps he wasn't honest enough, either with himself or the American people; the half-truths and untruths finally caught up with him. Also, he failed to see that the taping system he installed in the White House might prove detrimental to him in the long run, since it recorded everything he said indiscriminately; and in that he failed to see his own character as it really was. He was secretive, not open, and this hurt him badly, more, I think, than he ever saw himself. He could have overcome his weaknesses had he only realized them, and played against them; but he never did. Most historians seem to believe that he deserved to be impeached and removed from office. I was serving with the district attorney's office in Riverside County, California in the summer of 1974, when all of this was coming to a head. I was saddened but relieved when he finally resigned. In the end, one must say that his resignation was the best act of his political career; he got out when the system required it, with dignity and grace.

MR. THOMAS: And then Lord President Carl I succeeded.

THE LORD PRESIDENT: Yes, and it's a curious thing to wonder what might have happened if Congress had adopted a constitutional amendment proposed back in the mid-1960s to regulate presidential succession. There was some concern after the Kennedy shootings that at some point in the future the unthinkable could happen, and both executive offices, Lord President and Under President, might become vacant simultaneously, thereby creating a governmental crisis. The Speaker of the House, so their thinking went, might well be of the opposition party, and his succession to the office without an actual election would create a vast outcry from those being deprived of power. The resulting chaos could greatly hamper any attempt at administration. Two possible solutions were proposed; an immediate election whenever the Lord Presidency became vacant, or the appointment of new Under Presidents when required, with the advice and consent of the Congress. Both were discarded, however, for what must be regarded as well-reasoned objections; without the support of House Minority Leader Ford, nothing could be done. Consequently, when Agnew resigned in disgrace in 1973, and Nixon followed suit the next year, the Speaker of the House, Carl Albert, became Lord President.

MR. THOMAS: How do you assess his administration?

THE LORD PRESIDENT: He was the right man at the right time. After the chaos and uproar of the Nixon years, we needed a man who was quiet, understanding, down-to-earth, and Carl Albert was that man. As I recall, one of his first public statements specifically disavowed any attempt on his part to run again. He had originally intended to retire in 1977, he said, and his succession to the Lord Presidency had in no way changed his plans. He also said that he had never really wanted the job, but he'd do the best he could, since he hadn't any choice in the matter. Carl I was a wise man, in the sense of understanding his own limitations, and while he didn't accomplish many tangible goals during his administration, he did restore the balance between the executive and legislative branches of government, which was no small feat. His wide experience in the House helped him create smooth channels of communication between the White House and Capitol Hill; one got the impression that government in general was back on the right track. The only controversy that sprang up during his three years in office was the pardoning of Richard Nixon. Legal authorities remain divided to this day on the question of whether or not he did the right thing, but once accomplished, of course, a pardon can never be revoked, so perhaps it's after the fact; also, the fact that Albert was a Democrat tended to mute the public outcry. Nixon, as you may recall, escaped impeachment by resigning, but he was still legally liable for his actions. He and his colleagues were brought to trial during the ensuing months, and were all found guilty of various charges associated with the Watergate break-in and coverup. Just before Nixon was scheduled to be sentenced, Carl I released a statement saying that the poor man had suffered enough, and would continue to suffer, now that the public record had established his guilt before a jury of his peers beyond any reasonable doubt. Since the Constitution forbade cruel and unusual punishment, he now pardoned the former Lord President, who was free to return to his western retreat. Which, of course, he did, until his death a couple of years later of a blood clot in his leg.

MR. THOMAS: It was about this time, I believe, that you made your first foray into politics.

THE LORD PRESIDENT: Yes, Steve; in November, 1975, I'd heard Jimmy Carter speak before a group of attorneys, and I decided then that he had the best chance of getting the Democratic nomination, despite the large number of candidates that were springing up out of the woodwork. Since Carter's organization was quite weak in California, I offered my services to his campaign manager, and was made coordinator for Riverside County. I worked hard over the next six months, and although Carter lost the California primary to Governor Brown by a wide margin, the congressional districts in my area went predominately for Carter; my work was brought to the attention of the state-wide coordinator. I was eventually made his second-in-command in August, 1976, and when Carter carried California in the November elections, I was offered my choice of two or three jobs in various federal agencies. On January 20, 1977, Jimmy Carter became Lord President James VI Carter, and I joined the Department of Health, Education, and Welfare. I had already resigned my job in Riverside a year previously; and it was a simple matter to pull up my rather shallow California roots, and find a house in McLean, Virginia. Also about this time, I met my wife, and we were married shortly before I moved east.

MR. THOMAS: It must have been a very exciting period for you, sir.

THE LORD PRESIDENT: And indeed it was, Mr. Thomas. Washington had become rather stale over the past eight years, and the election of a rural Southerner with no ties to the political establishment set the place on end. Carter certainly knew what he wanted, and he proposed a series of reforms that didn't rest too well with the establishment. In the end, he was forced to compromise on most of his program, but he did manage to make the first significant steps toward improving the federal bureaucracy in several generations. My own career moved steadily forward, on several different fronts, since I was not only working for the government, but also pursuing my secret hobby of writing, under a pseudonym, of course.

MR. THOMAS: But I don't find any publications from that period listed in your vita, sir.

THE LORD PRESIDENT: No, you wouldn't, Steve, since I kept these things absolutely hidden from my superiors, who would have frowned on such frivolities; and also for another reason; a writer tends to draw his characters and situations from the people and social groups he's had direct contact with and I found my working environment a gold mine. Even though I disguised particular names, incidents, and personalities, the persons I worked with in those departments might have been able to pick themselves out had they known what I was doing. Some of my drawings-from-life were distinctly unflattering.

MR. THOMAS: Would you mind very much if I asked you what kinds of things you wrote?

THE LORD PRESIDENT: I'd rather not be too specific, Steve, except to say that my particular forte was the short story, and I wrote primarily science fiction. I've read and collected science fiction since the age of nine or ten. In fact, Dame Harrington, you may wish to note that I'm converting one of the upstairs bedrooms in the White House into my personal library, and may be forced to expand into a second room if I can't fit everything in. My collection numbers roughly 37,000 volumes, mostly paperbacks and other ephemera.

MR. THOMAS: If we could return to your political career, Lord President.

THE LORD PRESIDENT: Of course. I spent
four years in Washington, rising eventually to an under-
secretariat in the Department of Housing and Urban Development.   Carter was defeated in 1980, losing out to a
former California movie actor named Ronald Reagan.
I decided shortly thereafter to return to California. I prac-
ticed law for a year, and then ran for Congress from the 45th
district in 1982.

MR. THOMAS: And were elected.

THE LORD PRESIDENT: Yes. I'd maintained
some contacts with local political leaders while I was in
Washington, and it wasn't that difficult to renew them once
I was back in California.   Getting the Democratic nomination was actually quite easy, since nobody wanted it; in those
days, the Republicans were riding high.   Also, I was up
against an incumbent.   But I ran a campaign based on
bread-and-butter issues, and   won   when Reaganomics
began to have its difficulties.

MR. THOMAS: And were reelected again in
'84, I believe.

THE LORD PRESIDENT: Yes.   That was a
strange year. Ronald I was leaving office, after four un-
successful (and tiring) years of fighting with the economy.
The Democrats nominated a liberal senator, Donald Hansen,
and the Republicans went with Under President George
Bush. Then a group of dissatisfied Reaganites broke away
from the Republican party, formed a new political organization they called the National Caucus, and nominated a Southern Senator, Gerald Freeman. The resulting split gave the
election to Freeman, who carried most of the west and south,
while Hansen took the northeast, and Bush the midwest and
one or two western states. The key states turned out to
be California and Texas, and they both went to Freeman by
narrow margins. The Senate turned Democratic after four
years of Republican control. Gerald I was sworn in early in
1985, and was immediately faced with his first crisis, as
South Africa was finally invaded by its black neighbors,

Rhodesia, Mozambique, and Angola. This Black African League put together a fighting force financed by the Arabs, and entered Namibia, the first of its objectives. Unfortunately, the expedition seemed doomed from the very beginning, as the desert and South Africa's well-trained and -equipped army combined to destroy one fighting force and severely cripple another. The BAL withdrew its men to the peripheries of Namibia, and began guerrilla fighting. Then both appealed to the United States for assistance. I was a second-termer in the House at the time, and I can recall our astonished reactions when Freeman announced that the U.S. would send economic assistance and military advisors to the South African forces. I asked for the floor, and immediately began questioning the wisdom of sending more troops overseas; had not this policy already proved disastrous in the 1960s? But even as I was speaking, transport planes were speeding across the Atlantic towards the east, filled with American soldiers. I continued to speak out during the ensuing weeks, and even made a motion to cut off funds for the expedition. By Christmas we had 10,000 troops in Africa. Then the casualties started flowing back, and in April of 1986 I co-sponsored a resolution censuring the Lord President for acting without proper consultation with Congress. The public uproar finally reached the point where Freeman was forced to withdraw all the American "advisers," and greatly reduce military aid. Meanwhile, a popular California senator had died, and I was urged to run for his seat. I filed in March. I trounced my Democratic opponent in the June primary, and then found myself facing two serious contenders in the fall elections. Jeb Green, Bush's running mate, had refused to bury himself in a political grave after his defeat in 1984, and instead had begun organizing his new United Party at the local level, beginning with the midwestern states. He fielded candidates for offices in about 20 states in 1986, including California. His people did surprisingly well, taking one governorship, two senate seats, eight seats in the House of Representatives, and many local offices. Although I won my race, the National Party candidate was a clear second, the Republican fading to third.

MR. THOMAS: So you had finally reached
the national political scene, at the age of 40.

THE LORD PRESIDENT: I was sworn in on
January 3, 1987; I can remember the day as clearly as yes-
terday, cold, windy, with a light rain wetting everybody's
hair. Someone had decided to hold the Congressional swear-
ing-in ceremonies on the steps of the Capitol that year
(it's never been done since); one of my colleagues caught
a bad cold that developed into pneumonia: he died after
serving just two weeks, three days. Freeman's administration was rapidly going from bad to worse, as the economy
began sinking into another recession. The poor man tried
very hard, but he just wasn't skillful enough to cope with
one crisis after another. It must have been a living night-
mare for him. To make things even worse, the Republicans
had lost ground in Congress in the '86 elections, both to
the Democrats and Nationals, and were now in danger of
being eclipsed as the opposition party. In the midst of all
this, in the summer of 1987, a terrorist group intent on free-
ing Palestine from the Arabs seized an atom bomb in Iran,
and flew it to Italy, threatening to blow up Rome unless
their demands were met. Something went wrong with the
negotiations, or possibly the gunmen were unfamiliar with
the arming device; the bomb exploded, killing a half million
Italians, including most of the Italian government, and Pope
Paschal III. Freeman was blamed by some observers for
his intransigence in the bargaining, and the opinion polls
showed only a 15 percent approval rating for his presidency.
Rather wisely, I think, he chose not to run for reelection in
1988, and the National Caucus dissolved. The Republicans
nominated Alex Foresman, Senior Senator from the State
of Texas. I had sponsored a jobs bill early in 1988 that drew
much favorable attention from the press, and had generated
considerable public interest, and I was urged by many of
the party regulars to run for the presidency. I reluctantly
allowed my name to be used, and won several primaries
in the spring, although I never actively campaigned. The
leading candidate for the Democratic nomination was
Governor Silverberg of New York, although Albert Sanders, a senator from Illinois, also ran very well in the early

stages of the campaign. The convention was scheduled for July, and after the California primary, Silverberg had about 1300 votes, Sanders 1100 and I had roughly 600. Since it was clear to me that I had no chance at the nomination, I talked with both candidates about the possibility of supporting one or the other, discussing their views and positions on many different subjects, and trying to see what kind of Lord President either of them might make. I felt then, as I do now, that only a man with moderate views could be elected, and since Sanders was much more oriented towards the middle-of-the-road, I released my delegates, but urged them to support Sanders for the nomination. Al Sanders won on the second ballot, and when I called to give my congratulations, he offered me the Under Presidency. I accepted.

MR. THOMAS: And you won a resounding victory at the polls.

THE LORD PRESIDENT: Something like 55 percent of the vote, as I recall. Albert I and I took our oaths on January 20, 1989. Unfortunately, no one has ever managed to find very much for Under Presidents to do, except wait around for the Lord President to die, and that's a rather morbid subject from any point of view. I was kept briefed, and was asked to represent the U.S. on several different occasions overseas (I was in France, for example, for the state funeral of King Henri VI in 1990, and visited Dom Pedro IV of Brazil in 1992), but other than that we kept a cordial distance, and I was left pretty much alone to do as I pleased. I did make a number of trips to local party headquarters and functions, and in this way I met a great many politicos that I would otherwise never have known. Al was having his problems with Congress, since the Uniteds had increased their representation in the 1988 elections substantially, although their presidential nominee, Green, did not do as well the second time around. Still, between the declining reputations of the Republicans, and the ascending fortunes of the Uniteds, they controlled a majority of the seats in the House, and almost a majority in the Senate, and they made the most of it. Sanders was forced to veto a number of bills passed by Congress, and saw several of his most important proposals defeated. The situation got so bad that I was called over to his office one day, and asked to set up a liaison office between the White House and Congress. Since each party controlled one house, there was some basis for compromise on most issues, and I was able to mollify the opposition on several key bills, enough, at least, to get them passed. The United Party swept the congressional elections in '90, taking both houses outright, while Republican and National forces were virtually extinguished; rather ominously for both, several prominent Republican politicians switched their party registration to the Uniteds shortly afterwards, starting a trend that has continued to this day. In the spring of 1991, I was working in my office when I received an urgent telephone call: Lord President Sanders had suffered a stroke, and was in critical condition at Bethesda Naval Hospital. The cabinet met immediately, and asked me to assume the temporary role of Acting Lord President, which I did. I requested TV time from the networks, and reported the situation to the American people, emphasizing that I would exercise the powers of Acting Lord President only until Sanders had regained his faculties.

MR. THOMAS: There were no written procedures covering an emergency of this type. Did everyone agree that you should take over?

THE LORD PRESIDENT: For the most part, yes, although there were one or two members of the cabinet who felt that the entire issue should be postponed until the immediate crisis passed. I think they believed the situation might resolve itself if Sanders died.

MR. THOMAS: What were your own feelings on the subject?

THE LORD PRESIDENT: I was very hesitant to assume the role required of me, for several reasons: on the one hand, there really isn't any such thing as an "Acting" Lord President: you either are or you aren't, and unless Lord President Sanders died, I wasn't. Hence, I could only expect limited support for anything that I might try to do. My primary purpose was to keep the seat warm until the legitimate occupant returned, and not to initiate any dramatic new policies or measures of my own. I would be expected to handle any emergencies that might arise, but that's about as far as I could go. And if in fact I had tried to do anything else, I'm quite sure that the cabinet and virtually every other government agency (and possibly Congress) would have objected. In other words, I had no legal status, I was serving specifically at the pleasure of the cabinet, and my role was strictly limited. But, as luck would have it, I *was* able to accomplish something in spite of the situation.

MR. THOMAS: That was the famous Monaco Summit, wasn't it?

THE LORD PRESIDENT: Yes, Steve. For some years we'd been having difficulties with the Russians and Chinese on the Moon, as each super power kept claiming encroachment into its respective base territories. Finally, it started to get nasty when several pressure chambers were mysteriously punctured by pellets shot from a cannon. The Soviets had threatened a small war after one of their higher-ranking officers was killed, so I immediately proposed a meeting with People's Tsar Mikhail II Antonovich and Imperial Leader Wang in some neutral country halfway between our countries. They agreed, and Prince Albert II of Monaco volunteered his services. They even cleared out one of the casinos for us. The result was the Treaty of Monte Carlo, which specified the rights, obligations, and limitations of each party in outer space, and established a series of guidelines to be used by sovereign nations in colonizing other planetary bodies, whatever their size. The Senate promptly ratified the document, and several other countries have since added their signatures in the intervening decade. More importantly, perhaps, the rules seem to work, and we've had few troubles in space with the Russians or Chinese ever since. After three months as Acting Lord President, I was told that Albert I was well enough to resume his duties, and I reverted to my previous lazy existence.

44

MR. THOMAS: When did you decide to run for the Lord Presidency?

THE LORD PRESIDENT: It was quite clear to me that Sanders was unfit to run for a second term, and he confirmed that publicly in late 1991. After consulting with party officials, I announced my candidacy in December of that year. At about the same time, one of my oldest rivals, Jack Nelson, longtime Senator from Oregon, also announced. Jeb Green again indicated his willingness to try for the United Party ticket, but attracted little support; more enthusiasm was shown for Richard Rogers, Governor of Florida. Only one man, former Under President, Baron Conway, indicated much interest in the Republican label, and he was ultimately nominated in June. I'd been in politics long enough by this time to acquire both friends and enemies, and it turned out that I had more of the former, because I won the nomination on the first ballot in Los Angeles, soundly defeating Nelson by over 500 votes. The Uniteds nominated Rogers by an overwhelming majority. The campaign was fought over several issues of immediate importance, including aid to famine victims in India and Bangladesh, inflation, and crime, and I found myself forced to defend things over which I'd had no control (typical of the lot was the nostalgic slogan, "remember the one dollar stamp?"). I got behind in the polls, and I was never quite able to catch up, although the final margin on election day was only about 4 percent. Rogers was in, and I was on my way to a premature retirement.

MR. THOMAS: Had you made any plans prior to that time contingent upon losing?

THE LORD PRESIDENT: Not really. I'd briefly considered the possibility, but I had too much else to do, and there never was really an opportunity to review the various alternatives. I thought about getting a few novels out of my system, but that particular time of my life had passed, and I soon became bored with my attempts. I also considered going back into law, but I'd been so long absent from the legal scene that I was unfamiliar with recent legal developments, and didn't particularly feel inclined to catch up again. So I tried writing a few political scenarios, and enjoyed the research so much that I actually started piecing together a book on the subject; as you know, it sold very well indeed. This led to a second history, plus a series of commentaries in varous semi-scholarly reviews. I also started work on the Kennedy book at about this time, although I didn't finish it until 1998. The Uniteds took a drubbing in the elections of '94, and the Democrats regained control of Congress once again, for the first time in ten years. The Republicans by this point had shriveled to one or two Senate seats, and 10-15 House districts, and were no longer a factor. I was urged privately to run again for the Democratic nomination in 1996, but declined for a variety of reasons, mostly personal. Del Sanders, Albert's brother, became the Democratic nominee, and Rogers, of course, was renominated by the Nationals. Rogers used his incumbency well, and the Democrats were soundly defeated. The Uniteds regained the House. During this period I stayed out of the bright lights, preferring to enjoy the leisure time that I felt I'd earned; I did make a few public appearances, but kept them down to a minimum, primarily on the college circuit.

MR. THOMAS: What changed your mind about coming out of retirement?

THE LORD PRESIDENT: Well, Steve, I got a little bored, and I very much missed being at the center of things. So I put a few feelers out to some of my old party friends around the fall of 1999, and they were well enough received that I tossed my name out in January of the following year. Del Sanders tried for the nomination a second time, but I managed to come out on top. The United Party chose Alvero Douglas at its July convention. And as you're all aware, I won in the November elections by a large majority.

MR. THOMAS: In looking back over your career, do you have any regrets?

THE LORD PRESIDENT: Well, I regret that

I lost in 1992. (*laughter*) I supposed that everyone can remember times when he'd have done something differently. But hindsight is not a very useful tool when you're faced with an immediate problem, and you have to use the knowledge and wisdom that you have readily available to deal with it. If you've done your best, I can't see that you can be faulted for it. Yes, I have some regrets; but realistically, I try not to look backwards too often, lest I fall flat on my nose. Dame Harrington.

DAME HARRINGTON: Do you think racial unrest will cause you any problems?

THE LORD PRESIDENT: No, I don't really think so. We've become sophisticated enough in this country that racism just isn't an issue any more. I can remember the demonstrations and riots of the '60s and '80s and they seem now to have occurred in some other lifetime. Attitudes have changed, and while prejudice will exist as long as man exists, it no longer seems to be a factor in American politics. More of a factor, I think is the continuing issue of poverty which still falls most heavily on Blacks and Chicanos.

MR. PETERSON: How do you view the future of the space program?

THE LORD PRESIDENT: I think the next logical step in the development of space is the colonization of Mars. Our Moon bases and space stations have proved very successful in widening our perspectives and opportunities and I feel that Mars would prove even more valuable to the human race in the long term. Such a program would, of course, be enormously expensive, but the resulting technological breakthroughs would more than pay for our investment, as has been the case with every other space project we've undertaken. I also think we should explore the possibility of sending a probe to other planets or even to several nearby solar systems, realizing that interstellar probes would take centuries to reach their destinations. The challenge of putting together a mechanism that would literally survive the ages once again would have numerous immediate benefits to earthly civilization. We've pretty well surveyed our own solar system with various probes and landers, and have come to the conclusion that ours is the only planet with life. And only Mars and the Moon seem worth colonizing at this point. The next logical step is sending probes to the stars, and probing the stars for signals coming back. I would support any proposals aimed in this direction.

MR. THOMAS: When will the presidential coin issue be ready?

THE LORD PRESIDENT: I'm told by the Treasurer that the first coins, the five- and ten-dollar pieces, will be issued on February 1st, the others to follow as they're ready. I have a sample planchet stamped on the obverse with the new design, if you're interested. Ah yes, here it is (*he hands it over*).

MR. THOMAS: I wonder if you could hold that up to our cameras, sir, like this. How's that, Jack? Just a little bit closer, Lord President. Yes, right there, please. This is the new obverse of the ten-dollar coin, showing the bust of Lord President Lister. The inscription reads: "James VII, Lord President of the United States." Thank you very much, sir.

MR. PETERSON: Sir, Lord President Richard II is renowned for his patronage of the arts. What do you intend to do in this area?

THE LORD PRESIDENT: I've long believed that the government should provide some subsidies to artists, writers, and performers of all types, administered primarily on the local level, through state, county, or municipal agencies. The exact mechanism for distributing the funds could be worked out at some later date, but the basic principle of the thing should be established well in advance. There are a great many creative persons who've been forced into other professions because they couldn't make their talents pay. I reget this very much, because not only is the world deprived of their unique offerings, but all too often

48

their creativity tends to dry up for lack of exercise. Government-distributed stipends would provide assistance where it's needed most. We should, however, be very careful to formulate administrative guidelines in such a way that bureaucratic control of the projects is kept to an absolute minimum. We're not looking for poet laureates to celebrate the birthdays of the state governors with epic poems, and any attempts to impinge upon the creative freedom of the persons involved should be immediately squelched. At the same time, I think we do have a right to expect some end result from each person's stipend; if we're going to be acting as *le grand patron*, we ought, I think, to get something in return for the American public to appreciate. The idea, after all, is to encourage creativity and creative works, and I don't think we want anyone to get the idea that this kind of program is a free ride on the treasury. Yes, Mr. Thomas.

MR. THOMAS: Thank you sir. I don't believe we've said anything this evening about the crime problem, and the statistics recently released by the Federal Bureau of Investigation. The Lord Director stated in a press conference on December 16th of last year that the overall crime rate for the country had once again increased significantly for the 35th straight year, with murders up 6 percent, rape 2 percent, burglaries 11 percent, to name but a few. Your campaign speeches promised a hard line towards repeat offenders. What kind of proposals do you intend to make to Congress regarding new laws in this area, and what kind of policy changes do you expect to institute?

THE LORD PRESIDENT: This is a particularly difficult question, Steve, and I'm not sure I can really provide too many details at this point. I firmly believe that there are some criminals who will never be rehabilitated, no matter how long we try, and that these kinds of persons should never be released to prey on the public again. If that means building more prisons, so be it. Plea bargaining should be eliminated at once, and more appropriate sentencing should be introduced, with a wider range of tough options available to judges. Habitual criminals, those convicted of similar offenses more than two times, are obviously trying to make a career of crime, and should be discouraged from doing so with extremely stiff sentences, and no possibility of parole. A life sentence should mean just that. Organized crime can be fought in just one way, with large sums of money, and a police force specially trained to deal with the problem, and I propose we try both. Victimless crimes, such as the laws against marijuana that still remain on some states' books, should be reduced to misdemeanors, with appropriate sentencing. We ought to treat criminals the same way we treat all citizens, with fairness and justice, but we should not go out of way to grant any of them special rights or privileges.

MR. THOMAS: Do you favor capital punishment?

THE LORD PRESIDENT: Well, yes and no. I don't mean to be a fence-straddler on this question, but it's very hard to say that capital punishment is right or wrong in all cases. There are, I think, some instances where it seems the only appropriate answer to a particularly heinous crime; but even in those situations, it should be used with great restraint, with the Lord President making the final determination. It's the possibility of error that frightens me; we're all fallible human beings, and we all have the potential of making mistakes; to make a mistake with a man's life is something I'd hate to be responsible for. I can recall several cases from the 1920s and '30s where an innocent or probably innocent man was executed for something he didn't do. Does that answer your question?

MR. THOMAS: Well, yes, I think so, except that I'd like to know what crimes you would consider appropriate for the death penalty.

THE LORD PRESIDENT: Flagrant murders which involve deliberate mutilation, torture, or sex deviation; kidnapping with the murder of the victim-for-sale; terrorist crimes involving the death of one or more individuals, or the threat of mass murder (for example, the Rome affair);

50

political assassinations of high U.S. or state officials or foreign dignitaries; hijackings that involve death or injury to innocent passengers; treason (the real thing, not the spy dramas of screen and stage).

MR. PETERSON: During Lord President Rogers' administration, several laws were passed restricting press coverage of trials, at the discretion of the presiding judge or judges. How do you feel about this sort of action?

THE LORD PRESIDENT: I oppose it, and will seek to have that particular law revoked. Throughout our legal history, we have always made an effort to have the public represented at every trial in which a man's fate is determined by a jury of his peers. The television camera or the reporter is, in my opinion, merely an extension of this right, and indeed, carries it to its logical conclusion. By restricting the public's right to see judicial proceedings, we are in effect saying that the average American citizen is incapable of making a fair decision based on the evidence at hand.

MR. PETERSON: Those who advocate restricting media coverage say they must do so to protect the rights of the defendant. Too much coverage, so the argument goes, may so prejudice a particular case that a fair trial will be impossible to obtain in a particular geographical area.

THE LORD PRESIDENT: I don't believe it for a minute. Under such circumstances, I would go out of my way to be fair and open-minded to the accused, and I think that most Americans would follow suit. You know, Myles, I've been selected several times in my career to serve on juries, and I've always been impressed by the seriousness with which potential jurors take their duties. They were all very minor trials, of course, the kind that never reach the six o'clock news, but they were also the type where the police had an open-and-shut case. Most of these cases result in guilty verdicts when they actually go to trial, because the marginal ones tend to get weeded out along the way; either the judge drops the whole thing for lack of evidence, or the attorney for the defendant makes him plead guilty to a lesser charge. Once in a while the poor fellow tries to fight the charges, but they've usually got him dead-to-rights. Well, the cases on which I sat were all of this type; and yet, I remember very distinctly how meticulously we sifted through the evidence and testimony, looking for any shred of uncertainty in the prosecution's case. We didn't find any, and were forced to render a judgment of guilty, with a great deal of regret. The American people are not children, and we should give them credit for having the intelligence to take into consideration whatever special circumstances might pertain to a particular case.

DAME HARRINGTON: Do you intend to appoint any women to the Supreme Court or your cabinet?

THE LORD PRESIDENT: Well, I suppose so; do you intend to hire a male secretary to type your correspondence? I have several women under consideration for cabinet positions, but then again, I also have several men who might qualify, not to mention a couple of Australian sheep dogs. Dame Harrington, I don't try to select persons for administrative posts because they have green hair and fleas; it's quite the other way around, let me assure you, and their physical or sexual attributes are purely incidental. I try to pick the best person for the job. As far as the Supreme Court is concerned, I'll deal with that question whenever there's a vacancy. Mr. Thomas.

MR. THOMAS: While we're on the subject of courts and the press, do you favor the bill currently before the Congress that would grant the press immunity from revealing confidential sources to a judge or jury?

THE LORD PRESIDENT: I do in general, although I can envision several possible scenarios where such a privilege could and should be waived. Thus, I would prefer having some means of reviewing the situation by a higher court, which could then insist that the reporter's right of confidentiality be dropped if the circumstances warranted.

MR. THOMAS: Isn't this leaving a great deal of leeway to the judicial system?

THE LORD PRESIDENT: Not really. I think the general principle should be confidentiality, with the provision that special cases could be appealed. We should attempt to make the appeal process as difficult as possible.

MR. THOMAS: What kind of circumstances, in your opinion, would justify a waiver?

THE LORD PRESIDENT: A matter of life and death, certainly. You could say, of course, that any responsible newsman would gladly waive his rights himself in such an eventuality, and for the most part, I think you'd be perfectly right. But there are a few reporters who are not responsible, since irresponsible people seem to exist in every profession, and it is for these kinds of people that such laws are written, to protect the many and control the few.

MR. PETERSON: In looking back, who, of all your predecessors, is the one you most admire?

THE LORD PRESIDENT: Well, I'd have to say John Kennedy, I think, for several reasons. He wasn't our greatest Lord President, by any measurable standard, and the man certainly had his faults—he was as human as the rest of us. But he was intelligent, capable, and exceptionally likeable, with a remarkable sense of humor. I had the opportunity of meeting him not long before he died, and I remember every minute of that conversation to this day. He was a spell-binder; when he talked, you listened. As I mentioned earlier in this interview, I was greatly shocked by that tragic November day in Dallas, when Kennedy was shot and Connally killed; in a real sense, my own destiny has been shaped by what I saw and heard that afternoon. Strangely enough, whenever I've talked about it with others of my generation, they all seem to remember just what they were doing that fall day, when the first announcement came over the radio. For all of us, I think, it was a sudden realization of man's mortality. Here was this dynamic, charismatic leader, with his young, beautiful wife, and several small children, suddenly wounded near to death, and every one of us hanging over that thin thread, waiting morbidly to see if it finally parted or managed to hold on. We all wondered what would become of us if our leader died. And I myself have wondered ever since. It's the oldest question in history: do the times make the man, or the man the times? Did Lincoln suddenly surface because the times were ready for him, or did he make his own crawl to the top, thereby changing history forever? I don't know. I am convinced, though, that the world teetered that day on the brink of something, whether good or ill I'll never know, and that a gunman's slight waver when he pulled his trigger changed the course of history. And I wonder again sometimes—this is the science fictional part of me—whether there isn't a world somewhere where Kennedy *was* killed and Connally only wounded, where a Lord President named Lyndon Johnson served out Kennedy's term, where perhaps we never got involved in Vietnam. An idle speculation, I suppose, but one of vital interest to historians. I remember a curious incident that morning in Dallas, when Kennedy and his wife were just getting into their car; Kennedy got into the back seat for the first part of the trip, but after travelling a few blocks, he began complaining of pains in his back, and Connally offered to change seats. Kennedy turned him down, but Lady Kennedy insisted that he move up front, and he finally took her advice. They briefly stopped the cavalcade, and the two men switched positions. A few miles later, three shots rang out amidst the cheers of a sparse crowd, and both men slumped over in their places. Two of the bullets had hit Connally, splitting his head apart, and piercing his neck and shoulder, and one had continued on through his body to hit Kennedy, wounding him in several places. The Texas Governor died shortly after reaching the hospital; Kennedy remained in critical condition for a number of days. Lyndon Johnson was sworn in as Acting Lord President on a plane at Dallas Internatonal Airport, and managed to keep things moving until Kennedy returned to the Executive Office in 1964.

MR. PETERSON: If Kennedy had been killed

then, do you think history's verdict of his administration would be any different today?

THE LORD PRESIDENT: Oh, I'm sure of it, Myles. Consider for a moment the case of Lord President Abraham I, who was shot in the back of his head in April, 1865, just after the Civil War had been won. Lincoln was adulated as no Lord President ever had been, and that aura of reverence continues to this day: most historians regard him as one of this country's greatest leaders. But think for a moment: what would his reputation have been had his assassination occurred a year or two before or after it actually happened. A year earlier, Lincoln had been in serious political trouble; the Democrats, spurred on by the inconclusive nature of the war, looked like sure winners in the fall elections. There wasn't much reverence being shown the Lord President then: politicians, commentators, and even ordinary folk lampooned the Illinois bumpkin for his ungainly ways, homely face, and country-style humor. A lot of people resented Lincoln's success, a great many more resented his backwoods origins, and a number of others were just plain jealous. Let's take another scenario and say that Lincoln's guard at the Ford Theater had done his job properly, and John Wilkes Booth had been intercepted and arrested as he tried to enter the gallery behind the Lord President's box. Lincoln had nearly four more years to go in his term. The Radical Republicans controlled Congress, and were utterly determined to make the South pay a price for its treasonous conduct. Of course, in real history they had their way, completely overwhelming the hapless administration of Andrew II Johnson, and nearly succeeding in disposing of him as well. Would Lincoln have fared any better? Some historians don't think so; others say that he would most certainly have been more adroit in dealing with Congress, but still would have faced one confrontation and crisis after another. Remember, Andrew Johnson was only trying to carry out Lincoln's program for reconciliation with the South. Almost all of his proposals were actually borrowed from Lincoln's top hat. So you see, in both cases, Abraham I's reputation could have come down to us in completely different form, had he only died a little sooner or a little later. Kennedy's case is very similar. If Kennedy had actually been killed at Dallas, I'm quite certain he would have been revered by everyone far beyond his actual humanity. His defects and weaknesses would have been largely forgotten, and his good looks, humor, and decisiveness would have expanded to fill the gap. He would have been touted as the most beloved American Lord President of the 20th century.

MR. PETERSON: But, of course, it didn't happen that way.

THE LORD PRESIDENT: No, Myles, it didn't, and in a way I'm sorry it didn't; the man perhaps deserved better than he got. After he returned to Washington, Kennedy found things subtly changed. On the one hand, he encountered that certain amount of sympathy that one always receives with any serious illness or disability, and I think he found this difficult to cope with; after all, he'd always been a very active man, and he wasn't used to thinking of himself in quite those terms. And on the other side, Lyndon Johnson had managed in the interim to get a large amount of legislation passed that Kennedy had been pushing for years with little success, and I think he felt that Johnson had gone behind his back to do it. Johnson thought he was just doing his job, and he saw no particular reason why he shouldn't use his old legislative contacts to get a few things done. So they had an immediate falling-out, and the result was Senator Humphrey's nomination for Under President in the '64 convention. Kennedy rode his convalescent popularity into a second term, but it wasn't long before weeds began growing in Camelot. The legislative successes that Johnson had managed to engineer in early 1964 subsided, and the Vietnam War began growing bigger and bigger. All of Kennedy's advisers, both military and civilian, felt that the United States needed to support Vietnam, or lose all of Southeast Asia. So the war began escalating, we sent them troops, the troop levels climbed higher and higher, and soon we had hundreds of thousands of men in another country, fighting a war that wasn't really ours, with a steadily-increasing casualty list. Ironically, the 1964 campaign against

Goldwater had been based almost entirely on war fears, highlighted by the infamous commercial showing an atom bomb exploding, the implication being that Goldwater's election would lead to a nuclear confrontation.

MR. PETERSON: Do you think Kennedy could have found a way out of the Vietnam crisis once we had committed ourselves?

THE LORD PRESIDENT: Not very easily. The entire military establishment supported the war, as did most of the Lord President's top advisers. I think they all felt that the Cuban crisis had come about because America hadn't shown enough willingness to slug it out with the Russians everywhere they had given us a shove, and that we now had an opportunity to spit back in their collectivated faces. The real truth of the matter was never perceived: we were getting ourselves involved in a civil war that would never end until we withdrew, and despite our material advantages, in the long run we'd lose unless we were willing to kill off everyone living in the north. The French had learned that in 1954, and fools that we were, we were intent upon repeating history.

MR. PETERSON: But wasn't Kennedy responsible for American involvement? How then can you call him a great Lord President?

THE LORD PRESIDENT: Yes and no; the actual American involvement started with Eisenhower. However, Kennedy did escalate our military presence considerably, and he must, of course, take the ultimate responsibility for sending American troops overseas. I haven't called him the greatest Lord President of our times, but I do feel that he was very much a tragic figure, who was badly advised and badly served by those under him. That doesn't excuse his actions, but it does place them into perspective. Kennedy's popularity declined with the increased American presence in Southeast Asia, and by the time he left office in 1969, he was at his lowest point ever, a 25 percent approval rating. He retired to his estate in Massachusetts, and lived a limbo existence for the next 20 years, dying in 1989. History had overtaken him, and left him limp and worn out before his time; the few pictures we have of him from those later years show a thin, haggard man with hollow eyes, the portrait of a man haunted by his own past. If one could only change history . . .

MR. PETERSON: Lord President, I want to thank you for agreeing to appear on the Public Eye on the eve of your inauguration. I know you must be a very busy man, and we all appreciate you taking time out from a busy schedule to talk with us.

THE LORD PRESIDENT: Thank you, Myles; it's been my pleasure, believe me.

MR. PETERSON: This is Myles Peterson, speaking for the Independent Broadcasting System, and my colleagues are Steven Thomas of the Federal Cooperative Network, and Janet Harrington from the *Washington Digest*. Our guest tonight has been the Hon. James Lister, who will be sworn in tomorrow as James VII, 44th Lord President of the United States. Be sure to tune in again at this same time next week, when Don Agustin IV, Emperor of Mexico, will come under the scrutiny of the Public Eye. Thank you all, and good night.

Afterword

It has been almost six years since the first version of this fable, *The Attempted Assassination of John F. Kennedy, a Political Fantasy*, was published under the name Lucas Webb, and although it never made much of a splash, and is the least-known of my twenty-odd published books, it remains the favorite of my own work. I was therefore particularly pleased when Dr. Jeffrey Elliot read it, enjoyed it, and suggested that a revised and updated version might make a suitable text for political science classes; and even more pleased when he offered to do most of the revisions himself. It is pleasant to see one's name in print; it is even more pleasant to have someone else do the work.

At the time the original volume appeared, only one reviewer, Fred Patten, seemed to appreciate what had gone into the book, and what I was trying to do with it. The rest merely threw up their pens in puzzlement. "What is this business of 'Lord President?' " they said; "what's going on here?" In fact, I have made two explicit alterations from established history; the first, the most obvious one, is the assassination of Connally instead of Kennedy. Purely for the sake of argument, and not from any real personal conviction, I have assumed that the assassination failure had relatively little impact on history—the Vietnam War continued its development into that nasty little war that never seemed to end, Nixon was elected and fell on schedule, and the general course of events continued pretty much as they did in real life. This is one view of the flow of history.

The other is represented in my earlier, more significant change. I have assumed that John Adams and others who advocated establishing a monarchy during discussions on the proposed shape of the American constitution managed to convince George Washington to accept a modified, elective version of same, under the title of "Lord President." Adams believed that the president, being the head of state, needed some further ceremonial status and function to appear as equal before the rulers of Europe, and to stand above the people in his unique governmental office. In my version of American history, Adams was slightly more persuasive than he appeared in real life, and carried the day at the Constitutional Convention.

The consequences of this one small act ricocheted down through history. The French Revolution was not quite as violent as it actually was, not quite as radical, stopping short of abolishing the monarchy; Louis XVI was in fact deposed. as he was in real life, but he was replaced, first with the Dauphin, the minor Louis XVII, who was ruled by a revolutionary regency, and then later by the more pragmatic Louis XVIII, who, by the time he died in 1824, had firmly established constitutional rule in France. Napoleon Bonaparte was executed as a traitor when he tried to overthrow the legitimate government in 1799. Charles X was deposed in 1830, on schedule, when he attempted to restore the old royalist absolute rule, but was replaced by his grandson, Henri V (in real life the pretender Comte de Chambord), who again was ruled by moderate regents, and who was educated, not by his right-wing grandfather and uncle, but by upholders of the Constitution. When Henri died, to the great sorrow of his countrymen, in 1883, he was hailed as the citizen king, and was succeeded by his distant cousin, Philippe VII, heir of the Orleanist line. Louis Philippe served briefly as regent to Henri V from 1830-1841, and then retired to his country estate. A revolution in 1848 by a Col. Louis Bonaparte, a relative of the traitorous general, nearly succeeded, but was put down when the citizenry of Paris

60

poured into the streets, setting up barricades, much as they had done sixty years before.

Thus, the revolutions of Europe in 1830 and 1848, which in real life were ignited by the revolts in France, occurred with much less severity, resulting in less radical solutions to the problems of voting rights, land distribution, and the essential question of "who shall govern?" The solutions of France and England, and the earlier solution of America, provided the patterns for development of less sophisticated countries. The traditional monarchies of Europe were not viewed as obstacles to government by the people, but as the means whereby the upper classes could retain some semblance of rule while the real power gradually moved into the representative assemblies and parliaments. The retention of monarchies did not obviate the problems of modern civilization, but they ameliorated the solutions which actually were found. Even in Russia, where the revolution of 1917 overthrew the Tsar, the new head of government was called the "People's Tsar," and the reaction against the propertied and noble classes was not quite as severe as occurred in real life. Consequently, the civil war of 1917-22 never occurred, except for scattered clashes, and the economy recovered more quickly, with greater wealth for the workers accruing by the 1980s.

This particular scenario is not the only possible outcome of such changes, obviously, and it is certainly not meant as a utopia. As one alternative one might foresee, after the administration of Lord President George I, an increasing centralization in government under Lord President John I, gradually resulting in a virtual dictatorship of the executive, with the Congress reduced to a figurehead role. Then an unpopular Lord President, such as John Quincy Adams, could be overthrown in a military coup by General Andrew Jackson. By 1860, the pressures building up from an unrepresented people and from a series of incompetent rulers could result in the Second American Revolution (instead of the Civil War), ending in a populary-established governmental system based upon the parliamentary structure of England (to avoid an elected strong executive). One can play such games endlessly, and they are always fascinating to the student of history. Even in my version of history, Lister is far more open in his interview, both concerning his personal life, present plans, and past history, than any politician would be in the "real world."

The point of this book, then, is not to establish one man's views of what *should* have happened in history, or one man's views of the "right" political system or the "rightness" of any one leader or political philosophy. I have lived long enough to know there is no such thing. It is, rather, to get students thinking about the possibilities of life, about what one man or woman can actually do, given the right circumstances, given the proper assortment of personal characteristics. We are not all ciphers, wholly at the mercy of those who allege to govern us, whether politically, socially, or economically. We can and do make some difference in the world, positively or negatively (in my estimation, there is no in between). To make such a difference, one must recognize the possibility that it can and will happen, and one must be willing to take the risk of failing to achieve what one sets out to do.

History is no dead thing, no pallid assortment of facts and statistics and stale biographies—history is you and I, living in this moment, passing from the past into the future. It is the story of men and women like ourselves, great persons and little persons who lived lives much like ours in more primitive times, under circumstances at least as trying as our own, if not more so. By attempting to understand their stories, we understand a little more our own; by seeing the faces behind the looking-glass, we may also catch a glimpse of our reflected images. Like the two-headed Roman god of peace, Janus, by looking backwards we also look forwards. This—and entertainment—are my only purposes; if I have succeeded even slightly, I will be pleased enough.

Robert Reginald
San Bernardino, California
March 15, 1982

Study Questions

1. This book assumes that President Kennedy was never assassinated, and then examines what might have happened if he had continued in office. Three other presidents, Abraham Lincoln, James A. Garfield, and William McKinley were also shot and killed by assassins. How would the world have been different if they had lived? Conversely, how would things have changed if Presidents Ford or Reagan had succumbed to their attempted assassinations?

2. President Roosevelt was the target of an assassin's bullets in the month before he was first inaugurated, in 1933; the man sitting next to him, the Mayor of Chicago, died from his wounds. If Roosevelt had died, the Vice President-elect, John Nance Garner, would have been sworn in on March 4, 1933. How would this result have affected America's recovery from the Great Depression?

3. We postulate in this book that a black woman will become Vice President by the year 2001; do you think a woman or the member of minority race could actually reach such a high national office in your lifetime? Why?

4. The President in this book advocates freedom of choice for abortions, despite his strong personal objections to the practice. Should government be involved in legislating morality? Should strongly-organized religious or political groups attempt to impose their wishes upon government by supporting and funding candidates who parrot their views?

5. We often read in American newspapers stories about the monarchs of Europe; indeed, Americans seem to be fascinated by the subject. Why do you think citizens of the world's oldest currently-functioning democracy should be interested in foreign royalty?

6. No president has completed two terms in office since President Eisenhower retired in 1961. Why is this so? Do you see this trend continuing into the future?

7. George Orwell, in his book *1984*, postulates that by that year the world would have been divided up by three super-states, loosely centering on Asia, Russia, and the West; how closely do current world conditions approximate Orwell's fantasy? Do you think there will ever be a world state, with one government governing the entire globe?

8. If you were appointed dictator of the world for one day, what changes would you make and why? How would you make certain that the changes you inaugurate would still be here by tomorrow, when you are no longer in office?

9. There have been many debates throughout history over the proper form of government. Do you think the United States has the most ideal form of government in the world today? How do you think our government could be improved?

10. Consider your own life and the events in it, and remember one event that changed your life irrevocably as the result of something you did or did not do; how would you be different today if the opposite had occurred? Do you feel you have control over your life? If not, who does? If so, how?

11. Pick any occurrence in history at random out of a book or newspaper and construct an alternate scenario. Why do you think things would turn out as you would like them to?

12. Do you believe you can have an influence, positive or negative, on your government? On the world? Why?

www.ingramcontent.com/pod-product-compliance
Lightning Source LLC
Chambersburg PA
CBHW020650130626
46552CB00003B/1479